D0933950

THE CALL OF CTHULHU

Adapted by
Vincent Goodwin

Illustrated by
David Hutchison

Based upon the works of
H.P. Lovecraft

magic
Wagon

visit us at
www.abdopublishing.com

Printed in the United States of America, North Mankato, Minnesota.
102013
012014
 This book contains at least 10% recycled materials.

Original story by H.P. Lovecraft
Adapted by Vincent Goodwin
Illustrated and colored by David Hutchison
Lettered by Doug Dlin
Edited by Stephanie Hedlund and Rochelle Baltzer
Interior layout and design by Antarctic Press
Cover art by David Hutchison
Cover design by Neil Klinepier

Library of Congress Cataloging-in-Publication Data

Goodwin, Vincent, author, adapter.
  The call of Cthulhu / adapted by Vincent Goodwin ; illustrated by David Hutchison.
     pages cm. -- (Graphic horror)
  "Based upon the works of H.P Lovecraft."
  Summary: A graphic retelling of the classic horror story by H.P. Lovecraft, in which the monster Cthulhu awakes to threaten the world.
  ISBN 978-1-62402-014-8
1. Lovecraft, H. P. (Howard Phillips), 1890-1937. Call of Cthulhu--Adaptations. 2. Cthulhu (Fictitious character)--Comic books, strips, etc. 3. Cthulhu (Fictitious character)--Juvenile fiction. 4. Monsters--Comic books, strips, etc. 5. Monsters--Juvenile fiction. 6. Horror tales. [1. Graphic novels. 2. Lovecraft, H. P. (Howard Phillips), 1890-1937. Call of Cthulhu--Adaptations. 3. Monsters--Fiction. 4. Horror stories.] I. Hutchison, David, 1974- illustrator. II. Lovecraft, H. P. (Howard Phillips), 1890-1937. Call of Cthulhu. III. Title.
  PZ7.7.G66Cal 2014
  741.5'973--dc23
                          2013025338

Table of Contents

The Call of Cthulhu. 4

About the Author. 31

Additional Works. 31

Glossary. 32

Web Sites. 32

Found among the papers of the late Francis Wayland Thurston of Boston...

YOUR UNCLE, PROFESSOR GEORGE ANGELL, DIED.

PROFESSOR ANGELL WAS WIDELY KNOWN AS AN AUTHORITY ON ANCIENT INSCRIPTIONS.

MUCH OF THE MATERIAL WHICH I SORTED WILL BE PUBLISHED BY THE AMERICAN ARCHAEOLOGICAL SOCIETY.

BUT THERE WAS ONE BOX THAT I FOUND VERY PUZZLING.

1908 - Narrative of Inspector John R. Legrasse, New Orleans, LA, at 1908 A.A.S. Mtg. Notes on Same & Post-Webb's Acct.

1925—Dream Work of H. A. Wilcox, Providence, RI

CTHULHU CULT

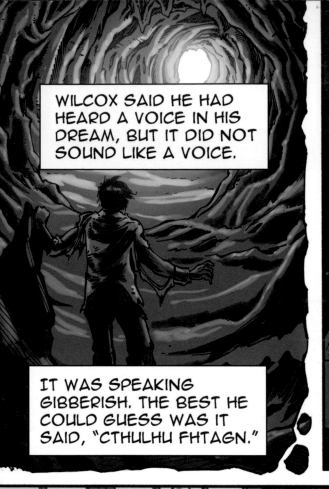

WILCOX SAID HE HAD HEARD A VOICE IN HIS DREAM, BUT IT DID NOT SOUND LIKE A VOICE.

IT WAS SPEAKING GIBBERISH. THE BEST HE COULD GUESS WAS IT SAID, "CTHULHU FHTAGN."

MR. WILCOX, ARE YOU A MEMBER OF ANY GROUPS?

LIKE A SECRET SOCIETY OR A CULT? NO, PROFESSOR. NOT AT ALL.

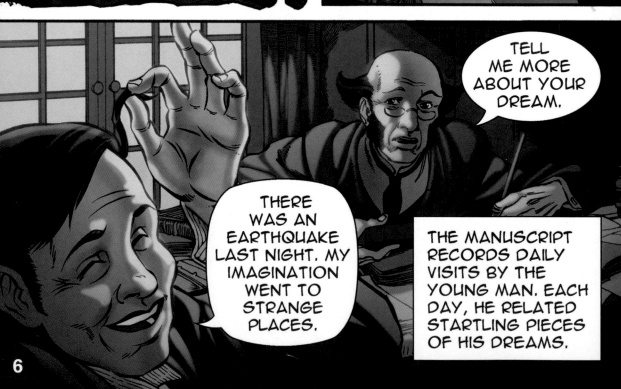

TELL ME MORE ABOUT YOUR DREAM.

THERE WAS AN EARTHQUAKE LAST NIGHT. MY IMAGINATION WENT TO STRANGE PLACES.

THE MANUSCRIPT RECORDS DAILY VISITS BY THE YOUNG MAN. EACH DAY, HE RELATED STARTLING PIECES OF HIS DREAMS.

THERE WAS ALWAYS A CITY OF DARK, DRIPPING STONE WITH A VOICE SHOUTING CONTINUOUSLY.

I HAVE BEEN ABLE TO MAKE OUT TWO WORDS FROM THE VOICE-- "CTHULHU" AND "R'LYEH."

ON MARCH 23, MR. WILCOX FAILED TO APPEAR.

INQUIRIES REVEALED THAT HE HAD COME DOWN WITH A RARE SORT OF FEVER.

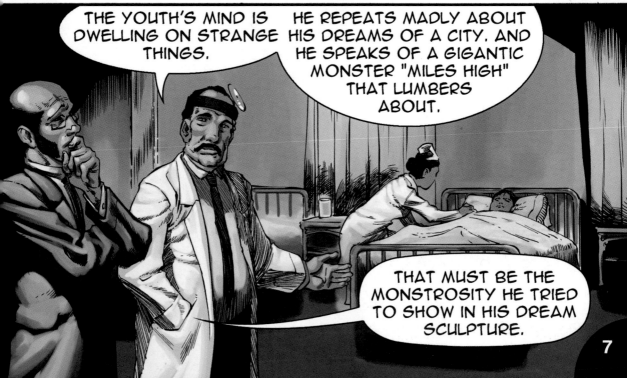

THE YOUTH'S MIND IS DWELLING ON STRANGE THINGS.

HE REPEATS MADLY ABOUT HIS DREAMS OF A CITY. AND HE SPEAKS OF A GIGANTIC MONSTER "MILES HIGH" THAT LUMBERS ABOUT.

THAT MUST BE THE MONSTROSITY HE TRIED TO SHOW IN HIS DREAM SCULPTURE.

BUT ON APRIL 2, WILCOX'S ILLNESS SUDDENLY DISAPPEARED.

CAN YOU TELL ME MORE ABOUT YOUR DREAMS?

DREAMS? WHAT DREAMS?

ALL TRACES OF STRANGE DREAMING HAD VANISHED WITH HIS RECOVERY.

THE DREAMS ABOUT THE CITY! ABOUT THE MONSTER THAT STANDS MILES HIGH!

THAT IS WHERE THE FIRST PART OF THE MANUSCRIPT ENDED.

BUT, MY UNCLE HAD COLLECTED DREAM DESCRIPTIONS FROM AROUND THE WORLD. THEY COVERED THE SAME PERIOD AS YOUNG WILCOX'S ILLNESS.

THESE REPORTS TOLD A DISTURBING TALE. FROM FEBRUARY 28 TO APRIL 2, 1925, MANY PEOPLE HAD DREAMED VERY ODD THINGS.

AND THE INTENSITY OF THE DREAMS WAS STRONGER DURING THE PERIOD OF WILCOX'S DREAMS.

MORE THAN A FOURTH REPORTED SCENES AND HALF-SOUNDS LIKE WILCOX HAD DESCRIBED.

AND SOME OF THE DREAMERS CONFESSED FEAR OF THE GIGANTIC, NAMELESS MONSTER.

MY UNCLE ALSO GATHERED NEWSPAPER CLIPPINGS FROM AROUND THE WORLD DURING THAT TIME.

The Times
SUICIDE IN LONDON

New York Times
"NIGHTMARE" EPIDEMIC

OTTAWA CITIZEN
PROMINENT CITIZENS SUFFER BREAKDOWNS

GARY HERALD
Doctors puzzled by rash
"ancient city" delusions

Chicago Tr
Mysterious dreams

IN SOUTH AMERICA, A FANATIC SPOKE OF A FRIGHTFUL FUTURE FROM VISIONS HE HAD SEEN.

AFRICAN OUTPOSTS REPORTED DARK MUTTERINGS.

ON THE NIGHT OF MARCH 23, CRAZED CITIZENS MOBBED NEW YORK POLICEMEN.

AND MORE THAN 500 CASES OF TROUBLE WERE RECORDED AT INSANE ASYLUMS.

SOMETHING STRANGE WAS HAPPENING BETWEEN FEBRUARY 28 AND APRIL 2, 1925.

AT THE BOTTOM OF THE BOX, THERE WAS A SMALL, CLAY TABLET.

THE TABLET THAT MR. WILCOX HAD MADE.

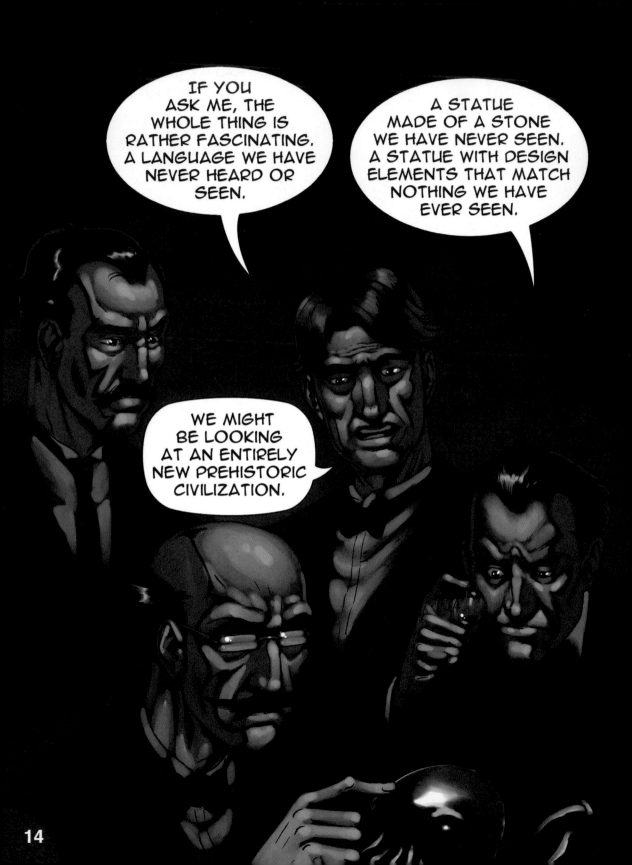

IT MEANS, "IN HIS HOUSE AT R'LYEH, DEAD CTHULHU WAITS DREAMING."

HOW DO YOU KNOW THAT?

WELL, FORTY-EIGHT YEARS AGO, I WAS ON AN EXPEDITION TO GREENLAND AND ICELAND.

THERE, I ENCOUNTERED A CULT OF ESKIMOS WITH A RELIGION OF DEVIL WORSHIP.

IT CHILLED ME WITH ITS BLOODTHIRSTINESS AND REPULSIVENESS.

THEY WORSHIPPED A STONE TABLET. ON IT WAS A HIDEOUS PICTURE AND SOME MYSTERIOUS WRITING.

15

YOUR IDOL IS GREAT CTHULHU.

WHAT CAN YOU TELL ME ABOUT CTHULHU?

CENTURIES AGO, OTHER THINGS RULED ON THE EARTH, AND THEY HAD HAD GREAT CITIES.

THE REMAINS OF THEIR CITIES CAN STILL BE FOUND ON ISLANDS IN THE PACIFIC.

WHEN THE STARS ARE RIGHT, THEY WALK THE EARTH. BUT WHEN THE STARS ARE WRONG, THEY CANNOT LIVE.

HOWEVER, THEY NEVER REALLY DIE.

THEY ALL LAY IN STONE HOUSES IN THEIR GREAT CITY OF R'LYEH. THEY ARE PRESERVED BY THE SPELLS OF MIGHTY CTHULHU.

THEY ARE WAITING FOR A GLORIOUS RETURN WHEN THE STARS AND THE EARTH MIGHT ONCE MORE BE READY FOR THEM.

"IN HIS HOUSE AT R'LYEH, DEAD CTHULHU WAITS DREAMING."

PRECISELY.

"PH'NGLUI MGLW'NAFH CTHULHU R'LYEH WGAH'NAGL FHTAGN."

WHAT HAPPENS WHEN CTHULHU AWAKES?

THE LIBERATED OLD ONES WILL TEACH HUMANS NEW WAYS TO SHOUT, KILL, AND ENJOY THEMSELVES. AND ALL THE EARTH WILL BURN IN FLAME.

17

MY UNCLE'S RECORDS HAD AN AUSTRALIAN NEWSPAPER STORY ABOUT A SHIP THAT WENT MISSING IN MARCH 1925. IT WAS FOUND THE FOLLOWING MONTH.

ON APRIL 12, 1925, THE *VIGILANT* SPOTTED A DESTROYED YACHT NAMED THE *ALERT*.

WE'VE GOT A SURVIVOR!

IT'S ALL RIGHT, MATE. YOU'RE SAFE NOW.

ON MARCH 22, GUSTAF JOHANSEN'S SHIP ENCOUNTERED THE ALERT. IT HAD BEEN TAKEN OVER BY PIRATES.

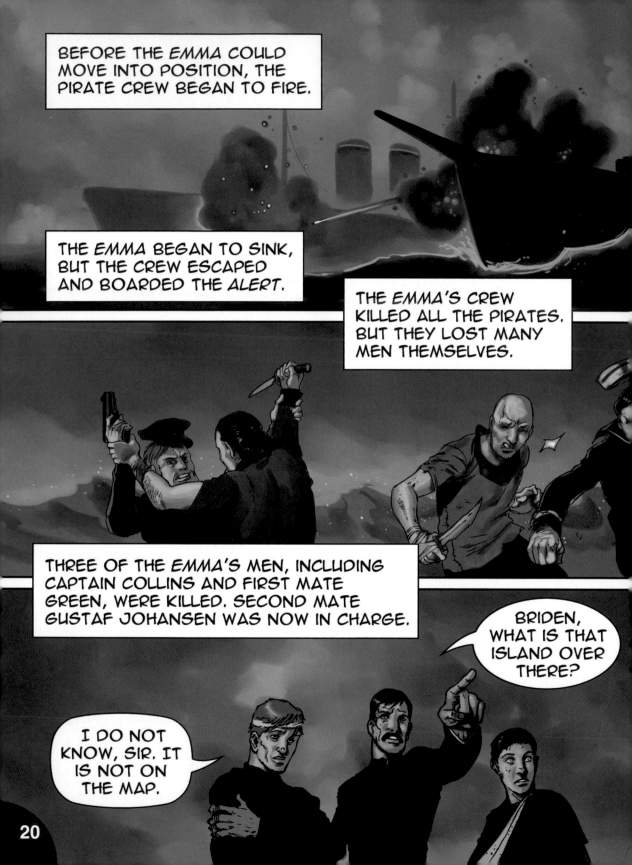

BEFORE THE *EMMA* COULD MOVE INTO POSITION, THE PIRATE CREW BEGAN TO FIRE.

THE *EMMA* BEGAN TO SINK, BUT THE CREW ESCAPED AND BOARDED THE *ALERT*.

THE *EMMA'S* CREW KILLED ALL THE PIRATES. BUT THEY LOST MANY MEN THEMSELVES.

THREE OF THE *EMMA'S* MEN, INCLUDING CAPTAIN COLLINS AND FIRST MATE GREEN, WERE KILLED. SECOND MATE GUSTAF JOHANSEN WAS NOW IN CHARGE.

BRIDEN, WHAT IS THAT ISLAND OVER THERE?

I DO NOT KNOW, SIR. IT IS NOT ON THE MAP.

ON APRIL 2, THEY FOUND SOMETHING.

SIR! OVER HERE!

WHAT'S BEHIND THERE?

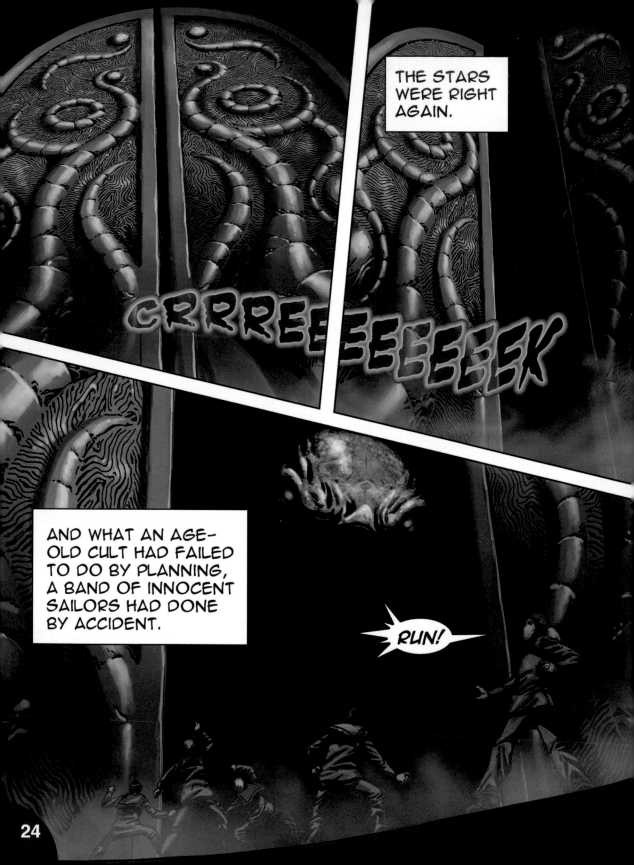

THE STARS WERE RIGHT AGAIN.

CRRREEEEEEEEK

AND WHAT AN AGE-OLD CULT HAD FAILED TO DO BY PLANNING, A BAND OF INNOCENT SAILORS HAD DONE BY ACCIDENT.

RUN!

AFTER THOUSANDS OF YEARS, GREAT CTHULHU WAS LOOSE AGAIN.

THE GREAT CLAWS SWEPT UP THREE MEN BEFORE ANYONE TURNED.

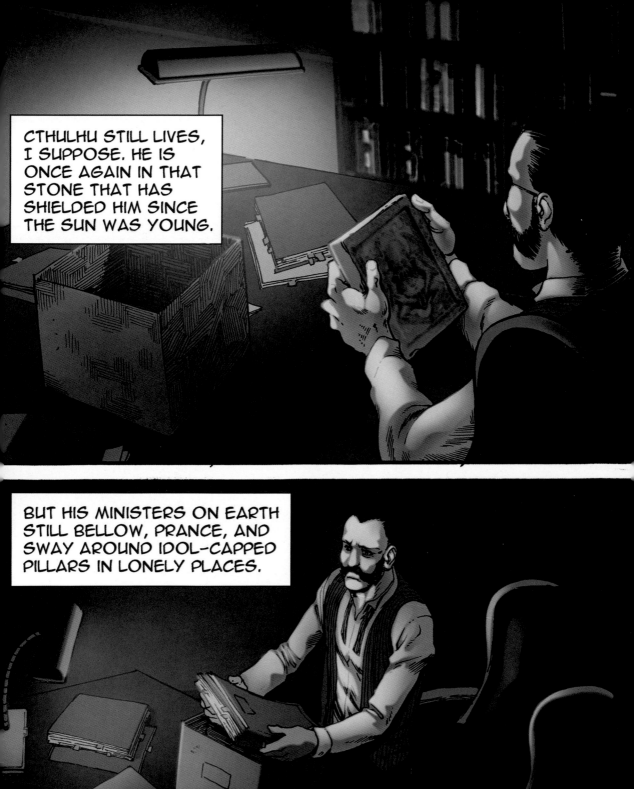

CTHULHU STILL LIVES, I SUPPOSE. HE IS ONCE AGAIN IN THAT STONE THAT HAS SHIELDED HIM SINCE THE SUN WAS YOUNG.

BUT HIS MINISTERS ON EARTH STILL BELLOW, PRANCE, AND SWAY AROUND IDOL-CAPPED PILLARS IN LONELY PLACES.

29

WHAT HAS RISEN MAY SINK, AND WHAT HAS SUNK MAY RISE.

The End

About the Author

Howard Phillips Lovecraft was born on August 20, 1890, in Providence, Rhode Island. His father was Winfield Scott Lovecraft, a traveling salesman. His mother was Sarah Susan Phillips Lovecraft.

Lovecraft was a bright child. He could recite poetry at age two and read at age three. As a boy, Lovecraft was often ill. When he was able to, he attended the Slater Avenue School. He later attended Hope Street High School but did not graduate.

Lovecraft learned mostly through reading on his own. His first printed work appeared in 1906. It was a letter to *The Providence Sunday Journal*. From 1906 to 1918, he wrote monthly astronomy columns for several other papers.

Lovecraft also composed poetry and fiction. His writing became popular when several short stories were accepted by *Weird Tales*, the pulp magazine. He soon was known as a writer of weird fiction.

On March 15, 1937, H.P. Lovecraft died after battling intestinal cancer. Today, he is often acknowledged as the inventor of modern horror. His works have inspired Wes Craven, Stephen King, and many other authors.

Additional Works

The Mysterious Ship (1902)
The Beast in the Cave (1905)
The Alchemist (1908)
Dagon (1917)
The Tomb (1917)
The Cats of Ulthar (1920)
The Dream-Quest of Unknown Kadath (1927)
The Case of Charles Dexter Ward (1927)
At the Mountains of Madness (1931)
The Dreams in the Witch House (1932)

Glossary

archaeology - the study of people and activities in ancient times. This is done by studying their remains, such as fossils, tombs, and art. A person who studies archaeology is called an archaeologist.

asylum - an institution that protects and cares for those in need, especially the mentally ill, the poor, or orphans.

cult - a system of religious beliefs or customs.

fanatic - a person whose beliefs or feelings about something are too strong, often beyond reason.

hieroglyph - a character in a system of writing using mainly pictures.

idol - an object or symbol of something people worship.

inscriptions - the lettering on a coin, medal, or statue.

pillar - an ornamental column.

tablet - a flat slab that is suitable for writing on.

voodoo - a set of religious rites characterized by a belief in sorcery and the power of charms. It originated in western Africa.

Web Sites

To learn more about H.P. Lovecraft, visit the ABDO Group online at **www.abdopublishing.com**. Web sites about Lovecraft are featured on our Book Links page. These links are routinely monitored and updated to provide the most current information available.